This Walker book belongs to:

_____

_____

_____

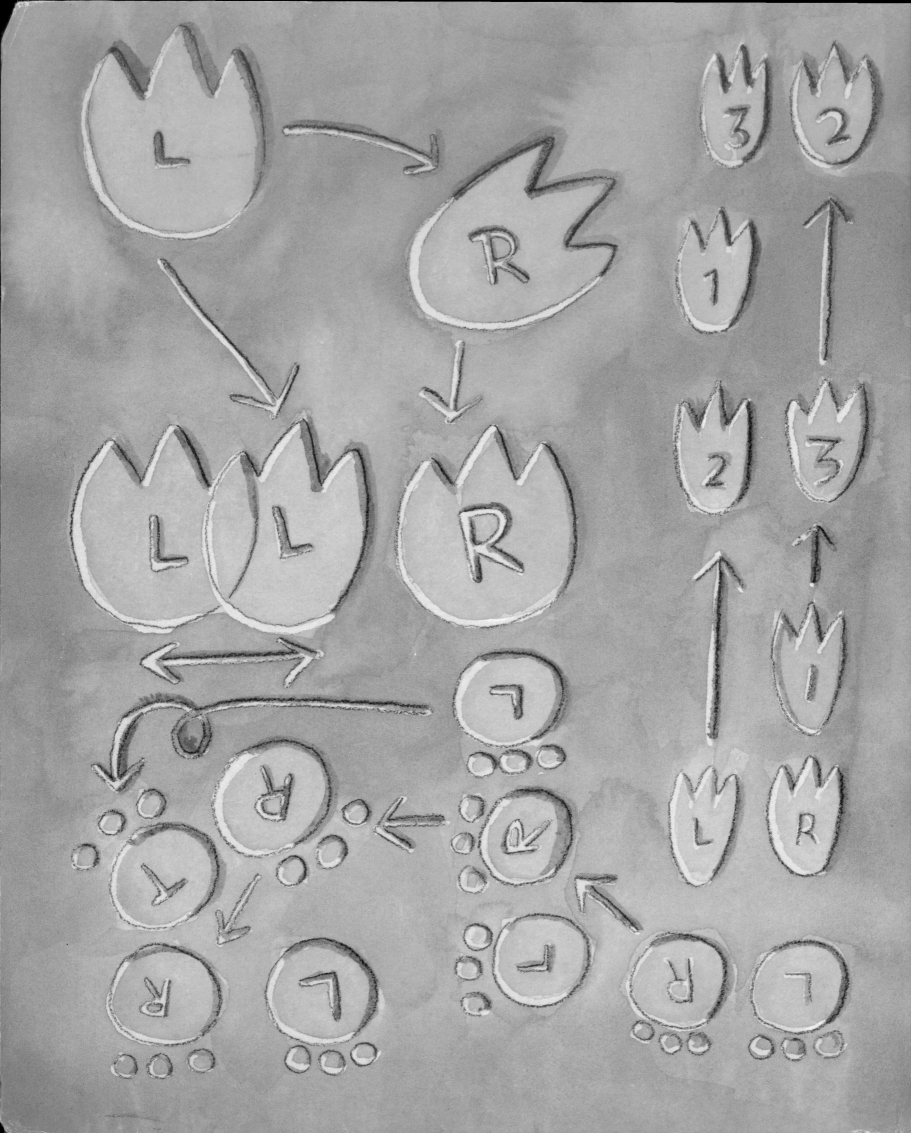

For Alex and Sam, with love
– C. D. S.

To Sarah, Timmy, Allison, Charlie and Nancy
– S. N.

First published 1997 by Walker Books Ltd
87 Vauxhall Walk, London SE11 5HJ

This edition published 2008

8 10 9

This book has been typeset in Cafeteria Bold.

Printed in China

British Library Cataloguing in Publication Data:
a catalogue record for this book is
available from the British Library

ISBN 978-1-4063-1268-3
www.walker.co.uk

Saturday Night
at the
DINOSAUR
STOMP

Carol Diggory Shields

illustrated by Scott Nash

WALKER BOOKS
AND SUBSIDIARIES

LONDON • BOSTON • SYDNEY • AUCKLAND

Word went out 'cross the prehistoric slime:
"Hey, dinosaurs, it's rock 'n' roll time!
Slick back your scales and get ready to romp

On Saturday night at the **Dinosaur Stomp!"**

By the lava beds and the tar pit shore,
On the mountain-top and the rainforest floor,

Dinosaurs scrubbed their necks and nails.
They brushed their teeth and curled their tails.

Then – ready, steady, go – they trampled and tromped,

Making dinosaur tracks for the Dinosaur Stomp.

Plesiosaurus paddled up with a splash,

Protoceratops ambled along with her eggs,

A batch of bouncing babies followed Mama Maiasaur.

A pterodactyl family flew in for the bash.

Diplodocus plodded by on big fat legs.

The last time she counted, she had twenty-four.

The old ones gathered in a gossiping bunch,
Sitting and sipping sweet Swampwater Punch.

Dinosaurs giggled and shuffled and stared,
Ready to party, but a little bit scared.

Then Iguanodon shouted, "One, *two*, three!"
Started up the band by waving a tree.

Brachio-, Super-, and Ultrasaurus
Sang, "Doo-bop-a-loo-bop," all in a chorus.
Ankylosaurus drummed on his hard-shelled back,
Boomalacka boomalacka! Whack! **Whack!**
Whack!

Pentaceratops stood up to perform
And blasted a tune on his favourite horn.

They played in rhythm, they sang in rhyme,
Dinosaur music in dinosaur time!

Duckbill thought he'd take a chance:
Asked Allosaurus if she'd like to dance.

Tarchia winked at a stegosaur she liked.
They danced together, spike to spike.

The Triassic Twist and the Brontosaurus Bump,
The Raptor Rap and Jurassic Jump.

Tyrannosaurus Rex led a conga line.
Carnosaurs capered close behind.
They rocked and rolled, they twirled and tromped.
There never was a party like the **Dinosaur Stomp.**

The night-time sky began to glow.

Volcanoes put on a firework show.

The ground was rocking – it started to shake.

Those dinosaurs danced up the first earthquake!

The party went on – it was so outrageous,

They stayed up well past the late Cretaceous.

When the Cenozoic dawned they were half asleep.
They yawned big yawns and put up their feet.

And they're *still* asleep, snoring deep in the swamp.
But they'll be back ... next **Dinosaur Stomp!**

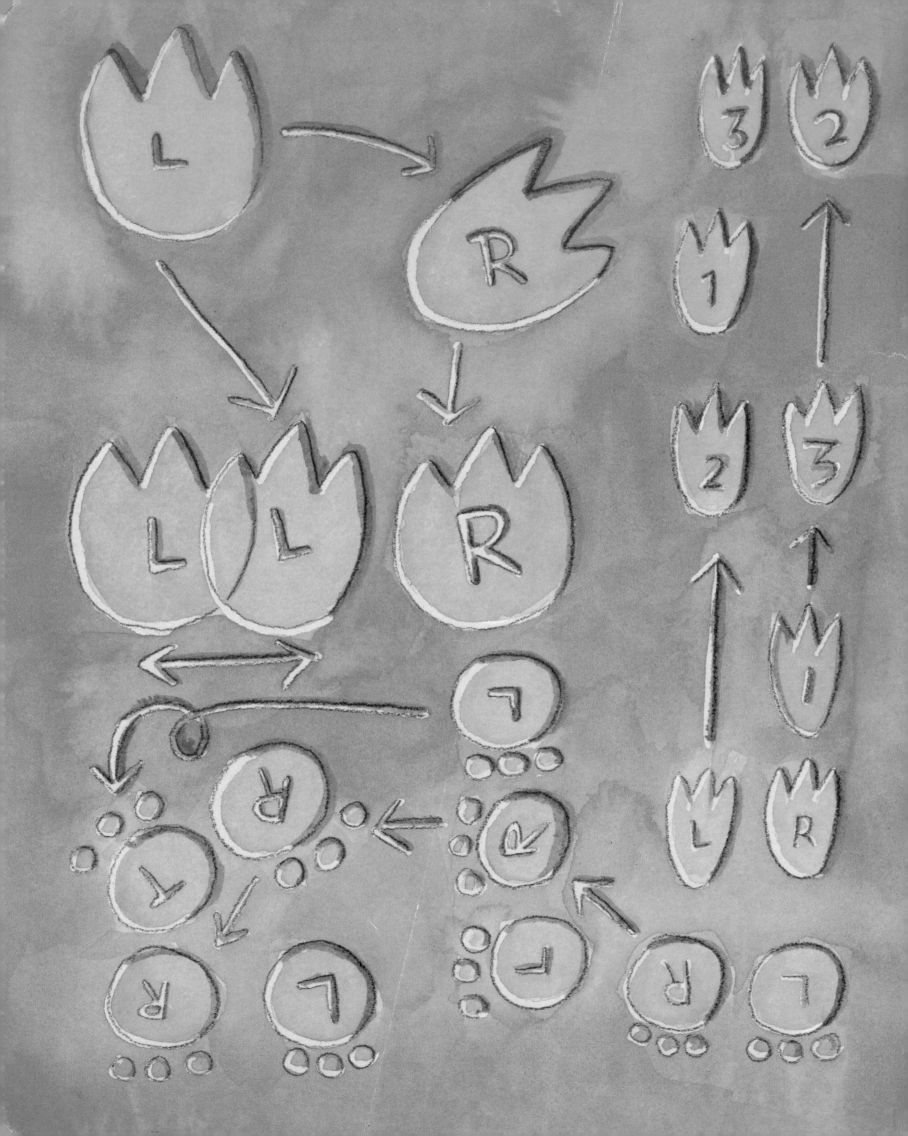

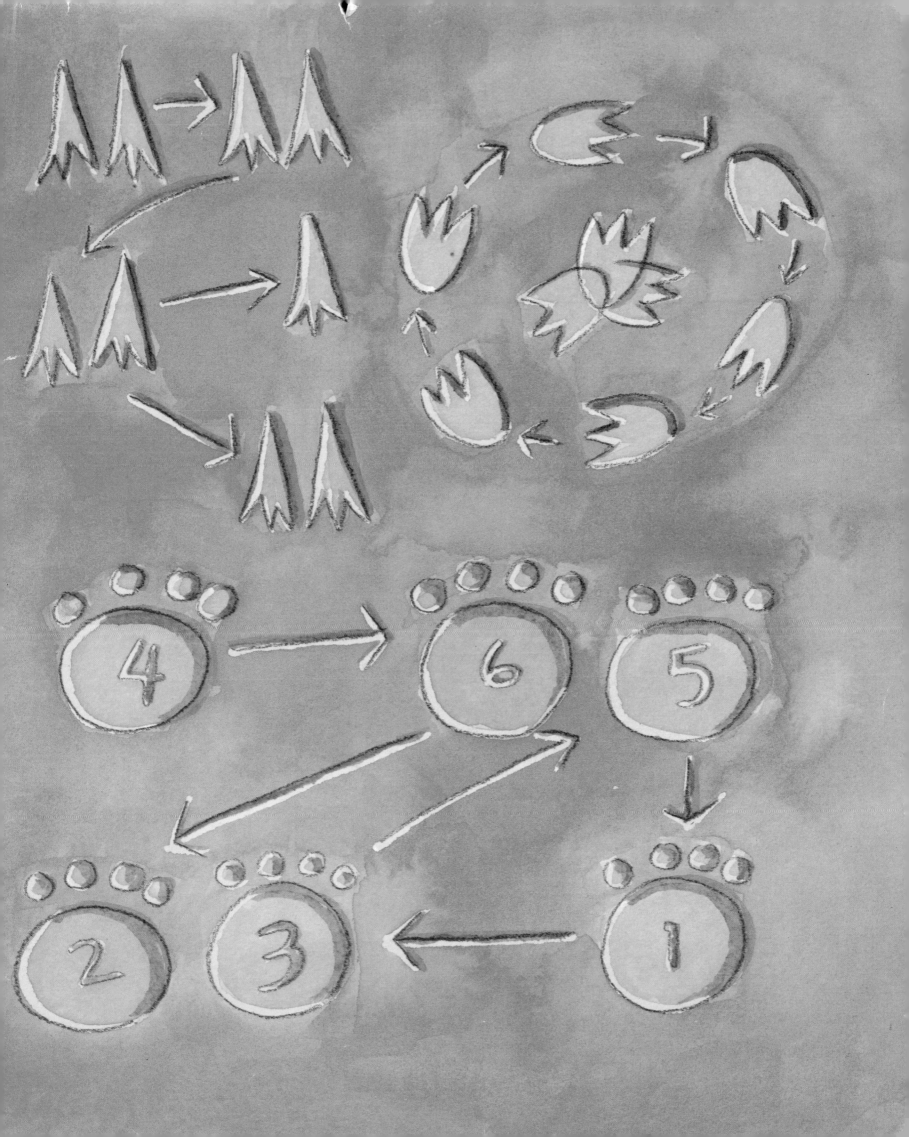

Another title by Carol Diggory Shields and Scott Nash

From the creators of *Saturday Night at the Dinosaur Stomp*

THE BUGLIEST BUG

Carol Diggory Shields   illustrated by Scott Nash

ISBN 978-0-7445-9813-1

Available from all good bookstores

www.walker.co.uk